THE VERY FIRST YOU

SCOTT STUART

Bright Light

Hardie Grant Children's Publishing

You are the **only you** in the world.

A you like the world's never seen!

Never before has there been one like you –

YOU'RE THE BEST YOU

THAT THERE'S **EVER** BEEN.

Nobody has ever **SMILED YOUR SMILE**,

or ran the way that you run.

The chances of you being

born as you are

were 400 trillion to one.

It's not just the shape
of your **nose**
or your **ears**,

or the **SHOES** that you wear on your feet.

Your heart sings a glorious song of its own –

THERE'S NO HEART THAT BEATS THE SAME BEAT.

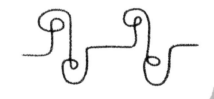

The **SPEED** that you move,

the **SPRING** in your step

and the way

that you land

in the snow.

The life you will live,
the path you will choose,
the places that you'll
want to go.

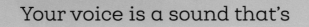

Your voice is a sound that's

never been heard –

YOU

SING

in your own

precious

tone.

The way that you dance has **never** been danced –
it's **your dance**, and your dance alone.

You're the first you who thinks like you do.

YOUR BRAIN IS **FULL** OF **IDEAS!**

Your **laugh** is unique, you've your own

FUNNY STREAK

and you cry your own heartfelt tears.

Your tongue has a **very distinct** kind of way

that it tastes all your **FAVOURITE FOOD.**

Whether it's cold or hot, small or a lot,

toasted, roasted or stewed.

You sleep your own sleep,

you snore your own snore,

YOU HAVE DREAMS
THAT **ONLY YOU** DREAM.

You imagine new worlds

that only you can,

and you build them

to your wondrous theme.

The way that you look at a painting,

the things you observe in the clouds.

You see the world in your own special way –

a way that should make you feel **PROUD.**

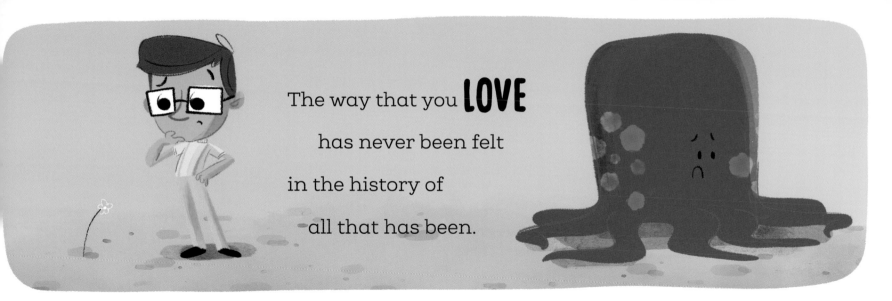

The way that you **LOVE**
has never been felt
in the history of
all that has been.

It lights its own spark,

it warms others' hearts,

and it makes people feel truly seen.

So what will you do
with this **gift** that is **you**?

WILL YOU BE THE

BEST YOU

YOU CAN BE?

Will you speak, will you shout, fit in or stand out,

will you do things that fill you with glee?

Whatever you choose
to do in your life,
here is **one thing**
that is true.

There's a hole in the universe built right to size, to be filled by the very first

YOU.

TO COLIN, THE INSPIRATION FOR THIS BOOK
& THE MOST SPECTACULAR YOU.
~ S. S.

Bright Light
an imprint of
Hardie Grant Children's Publishing
Wurundjeri Country
Ground Floor, Building 1, 658 Church Street
Richmond, Victoria 3121, Australia
www.hardiegrantchildrenspublishing.com

Text and illustrations copyright © 2021 Scott Stuart

First published 2021

A catalogue record for this
book is available from the
National Library of Australia

Hardie Grant acknowledges the Traditional Owners of the
country on which we work, the Wurundjeri people of the
Kulin nation and the Gadigal people of the Eora nation, and
recognises their continuing connection to the land, waters
and culture. We pay our respects to their Elders past, present
and emerging.

9781760508883 (hbk)

Designed by Kristy Lund-White
Printed through Asia Pacific Offset
Printed in Heyuan, Guangdong Province, China

5 4 3 2